My Ladybird Treasury
of
Stories &
Rhymes

My Ladybird Treasury
OF
Stories &
Rhymes

Ladybird

Stories and rhymes in this book were previously published by Ladybird Books Ltd
in *Teddy Bear Tales* and *Nursery Rhymes*.

All Ladybird books are available at most bookshops, supermarkets and newsagents, or can be ordered direct from:
Ladybird Postal Sales PO Box 133 Paignton TQ3 2YP England
Telephone: (+44) 01803 554761 *Fax:* (+44) 01803 663394

A catalogue record for this book is available from the British Library

Published by Ladybird Books Ltd
A subsidiary of the Penguin Group
A Pearson Company
© LADYBIRD BOOKS LTD MCMXCVIII
Birthday Bear © Georgina Russell

LADYBIRD and the device of a Ladybird are trademarks of Ladybird Books Ltd Loughborough Leicestershire UK

Contents

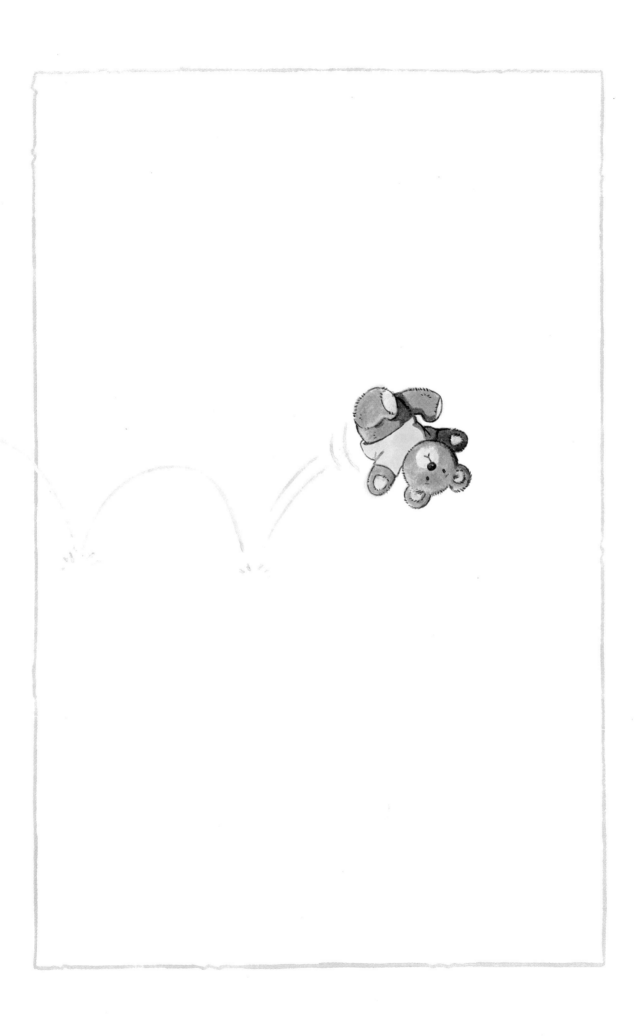

TEDDY
BEAR
TALES

About the stories and rhymes...

Children love teddy bears. Teddies have a special place in the hearts of their young owners, sharing hopes and dreams, secrets and worries. And as all young owners know, teddy bears have lots of adventures! This collection of nineteen stories and rhymes features a teddy who kept being left behind and some teddies who had fun when their young owners were fast asleep.

Contents

What a Teddy Bear Needs

In a toy shop, on a shelf, sat a row of brand-new teddy bears. They all had fluffy brown fur. They all had big button noses. They all had bright red ribbons round their necks. And they were all smiling.

Except for Eddy Teddy. Eddy Teddy never smiled.

"You need to smile," the other bears told him. "If you don't smile, no one will ever want to take you home."

"I don't need to smile," Eddy said proudly. "I have the fluffiest fur and the biggest nose and the brightest ribbon. I'm the finest teddy bear in this shop."

Just then, a little boy and his mother came into the shop. All the teddy bears sat up straight and smiled their biggest smiles. All except Eddy Teddy. He just sat there.

"I want that one," the little boy told his mother. He pointed to the bear just to the left of Eddy.

What a silly boy, thought Eddy. *I've got fluffier fur than that bear!*

Then a little girl and her father came into the shop. "Please, may I have that bear?" she asked her father. She pointed to the bear just to the right of Eddy.

What a foolish girl, thought Eddy. *That bear's nose is much smaller than mine!*

More and more boys and girls came into the shop. One by one, they each picked a teddy bear. But no one picked Eddy Teddy. Soon he was all alone on the shelf.

I'm not going to sit here and wait any longer, Eddy decided. *I'll go out and find someone to take me home!*

He hopped down from the shelf and left the shop.

Across the road, there was a big park where boys and girls were playing. Eddy saw one little boy playing with a very old teddy bear.

"Hello," said Eddy, walking right up to the boy. "My name is Eddy Teddy, and I will be your new bear."

"No, thank you," said the little boy. "I already have a teddy bear."

"But I'm a much better teddy bear!" Eddy said. "I have the fluffiest fur and the biggest nose and the brightest ribbon. I'm the finest teddy bear in the world!"

"But my teddy bear has something you don't have," said the boy. And he walked away, hugging his old teddy bear.

Then Eddy saw another little boy playing with a tatty old teddy bear.

"Hello," said Eddy. "Wouldn't you like a nice new teddy bear?"

"No, thank you," the boy said. "I'm happy with my own teddy bear."

"But your teddy bear doesn't have fluffy fur, or a big button nose, or a red ribbon," Eddy told him.

"I don't care," the boy said. "He's got something better."

15

Then Eddy saw a little girl playing all alone. She was the prettiest girl Eddy had ever seen. She had yellow hair and big blue eyes. He hurried over to her.

"Hello," said Eddy. "Do you want a teddy bear?"

"Yes, I do," said the little girl.

"Well, here I am!" said Eddy.

"No, thank you," the little girl said. "You're not the right teddy bear for me."

"Why not?" asked Eddy. "I have the fluffiest fur and the biggest nose and the brightest ribbon!"

"But you don't have what a teddy bear really needs," the little girl said sadly.

Eddy was puzzled. He was sure he had everything a teddy bear needed.

Then Eddy saw a rose bush. *That must be what I need,* he thought. *A big red rose for my bright red ribbon.* So he jumped into the rose bush to get the biggest rose.

"Ouch! Ouch! Help!" The thorns pricked Eddy all over. He was stuck inside the bush and he couldn't get out.

The little girl with the yellow hair grabbed Eddy's ears and pulled him free.

"Oh, dear," she said. "You've lost your button nose."

That wasn't all. Stuck to the thorns were bits and pieces of Eddy's fur. And waving from a branch was his bright red ribbon.

"Oh, no!" Eddy cried. He turned away from the little girl and ran all the way back to the toy shop.

On the shelf sat a row of brand-new teddy bears. When they saw Eddy, they shook their heads. "You look terrible!" they said.

Eddy wanted to cry. Now no one would ever want to take him home.

Just then the shop door opened. In walked the yellow-haired little girl with her mother.

All the teddy bears sat up straight and smiled. Except for Eddy Teddy. He hung his head in shame.

"Hello," said the little girl.

Eddy looked up. The little girl was standing right in front of him. She smiled.

And Eddy couldn't help himself. He smiled right back.

"That's the teddy bear I want," the little girl said.

Her mother was surprised. "But he doesn't have fluffy fur or a red ribbon or a button nose," she said. "Why do you want him?"

"Because he has the nicest smile," the little girl said, taking Eddy down from the shelf.

Then Eddy knew what a teddy bear really needs. A teddy bear doesn't need the fluffiest fur or the biggest nose or the brightest ribbon. All a teddy bear needs is a great big smile.

And as the little girl hugged him tightly, Eddy Teddy knew that he would go on smiling for ever.

Seven Sporty Bears

Monday's bear runs far and wide,
Tuesday's bear can bike and ride.

Wednesday's bear plays ball with me,
Thursday's bear can climb a tree.

Friday's bear *will* jump in puddles,
Saturday's bear is best at cuddles.

But Sunday's bear, I'm proud to say,
Has just scored a goal…
Hip, hip, HOORAY!

Teddy and the Talent Show

Teddy and Tom were excited. They were about to watch a talent show.

"I do hope there'll be a trick cyclist," said Tom.

Well, I want to see some real magic, thought Teddy. And he peered out from his tip-up seat.

The first act was a group of singers. They were very good, and Teddy tapped his paw while Tom hummed to the music.

Next came a comedian. Tom couldn't stop laughing at the jokes. And Teddy nearly fell off his seat.

Then Tom got his wish, and a trick cyclist sped onto the stage.

"Wow!" whispered Tom. "I can barely balance on two wheels, let alone one."

And I still need three and a knee, thought Teddy.

The next act was a troupe of dancers. Teddy and Tom looked at each other and yawned. But there was still one act to follow.

"Now, last," boomed the voice of the presenter, "but by no means least," he added cheerfully, "I give you… *Malcolm the Magician!*"

Teddy sat bolt upright. And when Malcolm asked for a volunteer from the audience, somehow Teddy's arm shot up with all the rest.

Malcolm pretended to take a long time choosing. "The young man in the striped dungarees," he announced at last.

First Teddy was put in a special box.

"*Oooooob,*" went the audience. It looked just as if Malcolm was sawing Teddy in two!

Then he made him disappear...

and reappear with a rabbit.

In fact, Teddy helped Malcolm with all his tricks. At the end of the act the applause was deafening.

That night Mum asked Tom if he had enjoyed the show.

"Oh, Mum," cried Tom, "it was... *magic!*"

And Teddy couldn't help but agree.

The Teddy Bear
Who Couldn't Do Anything

The teddy bear rested his head on the pillow and looked at the toy shelf. The other toys didn't say hello, or smile, or even nod. They never paid any attention to him. They thought he was just a silly old bear who didn't know how to do anything.

Perhaps they're right, thought the teddy bear, looking at the other toys. *The soldier knows how to march. The ballerina knows how to dance. The monkey can play the drum. But all I can do is lie here.*

Up on the shelf, the soldier was getting ready to march. He straightened his shoulders and stood tall as he stepped forward.

The teddy bear watched the shiny soldier march proudly across the shelf. He swung his arms and tapped his heels and turned smartly each time he came to the edge.

"Perhaps I can stand straight and tall and march like the soldier," said the teddy bear, sitting up. "In fact, I'm *sure* I can."

The toy soldier stopped marching and stared at the bear. "What did you say?" he asked.

"Well," said the teddy bear quietly, because suddenly he wasn't so sure of himself, "I could try."

The teddy bear rolled off the bed and tried to march. But his legs were too fat and his tummy was too big. He took three small steps and fell down.

The other toys laughed as the bear climbed back onto the bed.

Then the ballerina began to dance. Round and round she twirled.

The teddy bear tried to dance like the ballerina, but he was much too clumsy. He fell down with a thud, and felt very foolish indeed.

There must be something I can do, the
teddy bear thought as he pulled
himself back onto the bed.
But as hard as he tried, he
couldn't think of a single thing.

Just then the monkey stepped forward
and started to play his drum. *Tap, tap,*
went the drum. *Tap, tap, tap, tap, tap, tap.*

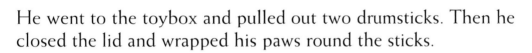

The teddy bear sat up and listened.
"I can do that," he said. "I can make
a drumming sound like that."

He went to the toybox and pulled out two drumsticks. Then he
closed the lid and wrapped his paws round the sticks.

Tap, tap, went the drumsticks on the toybox lid. The teddy bear
smiled. At last he had found something he could do.

But then the sticks slid out of his fat little paws and fell to the floor.

The teddy bear shook his head and sat down in the corner.
"It's no use," he sighed. "I really can't do anything special."

He sat in the corner for a long time, while the other toys marched and played and danced. Then he climbed back into bed and slid down under the covers.

When the sun set and the room grew dark, the little soldier led the ballerina and the monkey back to their places on the shelf. Soon it would be time for the boy to come into the room.

At last the boy turned on the light.
He walked over to the toy shelf.

The soldier stood tall and proud.

The monkey held his drumsticks tightly.

The ballerina was on her toes, ready to dance.

But the boy shook his head. He walked over to the bed and looked on his pillow. Then he looked under the bed. The boy's face grew worried and sad.

Finally the boy got into bed. But he couldn't sleep. Something was wrong.

And then the boy's toe felt something—something soft and round and fat and nice. He reached down, deep under the covers, and found… his teddy bear.

The boy hugged the bear and was happy.

And the bear who couldn't do anything but hug was happy, too.

A Stitch in Time

"Cheer up, Teddy!" began Rabbit.

"It's a lovely, sunny day," went on Dog.

"And you should be happy!" finished Cat.

"But I *am* happy," Teddy told them. "It's just that my mouth turns down at the corners. And I can't do anything about it."

"Good heavens!" cried Cat. *She* had a smile as wide as her face.

"Do you mean you were *made* that way?" grinned Dog and Rabbit together.

Teddy nodded sadly. "However happy I feel inside," he explained, "I always *look* miserable. If only I had just a small smile, then I'm sure Boy would spend more time with me."

That night, when Teddy was asleep, Rabbit, Dog and Cat lay awake. At last they came up with a plan.

Next day they told Teddy what he must do.

"Will it hurt?" he asked.

Rabbit, Dog and Cat shook their heads. "Not much," they said.

After supper Boy had his bath.

"Just look at this T-shirt!" cried his mum. "It's almost torn in half."

And with that, she opened the bathroom door and threw the T-shirt across the hallway. It landed in the mending pile.

"*Now!*" cried Rabbit, Dog and Cat.

Teddy leaned over the edge of the bed. "*Ouch!*" He bounced onto the floor, across the hallway and straight on top of the mending pile.

When Boy woke up next morning, Teddy was propped up at the end of his bed. Rabbit, Dog and Cat grinned and waited.

"And what are *you* smiling about?" Boy asked Teddy.

Teddy didn't say a word. He just smiled back.

"Come on," cried Boy suddenly. He grabbed Teddy and leapt out of bed.

"It's a lovely, sunny day. And we're going to play outside together... *all morning!*"

It Was Teddy!

Carl was a careless little boy. But he didn't like to admit it.

So, when he turned on the taps and flooded the bathroom, he wouldn't own up. "It was Teddy!" he told his parents.

The same thing happened when Carl took an ice cream out of the freezer, and then left it to melt.

"What a waste!" said Mum.

"What a *careless* Teddy!" sighed Carl.

Then one day Carl accidentally hurled a ball through Mrs Weaver's window.

"*Naughty* Teddy!" announced naughty Carl.

"Teddy has been causing a *lot* of trouble," said Dad. So he decided to have a talk with Carl's teacher.

Now, Carl and Teddy were still new boys at school. But Carl enjoyed school, and he worked hard.

"Next week," Miss Mulberry told the children, "we are having an important visitor. I want you all to make her a nice picture."

Carl painted his best picture ever. Miss Mulberry put it up on the wall along with the others.

When the important visitor arrived, she was impressed. "What wonderful paintings!" she exclaimed. Then she took a closer look and pointed to Carl's. "Who painted *this* one?" she asked. "It's outstanding!"

Carl squirmed with pride, and Miss Mulberry smiled across the room. "It was Teddy!" she told the visitor.

That evening Carl took a glass of milk up to his bedroom. But he soon came down again.

"Sorry, " said Carl. "I've spilt my milk and made a mess."

Mum and Dad looked amazed. "Who taught you to own up?" they asked.

Carl beamed at his parents. Then he told them, "It was Teddy!"

Pawmarks

There are pawmarks on the table,
There are pawmarks on the chairs.
There are pawmarks in the hallway,
As well as up the stairs!

There are pawmarks in the bathroom,
There are pawmarks on the mat.
There are pawmarks on the aftershave –
Dad won't think much of *that*!

There are pawmarks in the bedroom,
There are pawmarks in the bed.
There are pawmarks on my nightie
In several shades of red.

Now, each and every pawmark
Came from a bear called Sid –
And all because the finger paints
Were left without a lid!

Birthday Bear

"That's the end of your story, Sally," said Mum. "Now snuggle down with Bear and go to sleep."

"I'm too excited to sleep," said Sally. "I can't wait until tomorrow."

"I know," said Mum. "There are going to be lots of surprises."

Bear listened with sudden interest. Surprises! He liked surprises, too.

Sally lay awake for a long time, tossing and turning and thinking and wondering. But at last she drifted off to sleep.

Bear, however, was still doing a lot of thinking and wondering of his own.

As soon as everyone was asleep, Bear slipped out of Sally's arms and slid down onto the floor.

"I'll start with the cupboard under the stairs," he said to himself. "That's a good hiding place for surprises."

It was dark and crowded in the cupboard, so Bear had to rummage around with his paws.

"Coats and scarves, boots and shoes, cans of old paint, umbrellas…" he muttered. "But no sign of any surprises."

He rummaged some more.

"Brushes and brooms, a teapot, a beach ball, an old hat… Oh! And a big parcel wrapped in pretty paper and tied with a ribbon!"

Bear paused…

"A parcel... Parcels mean presents, and presents mean surprises. So this must be a surprise," he decided.

He looked longingly at the parcel, wondering what was inside. But he didn't open it. "If I open it, it won't be a surprise any longer," he said to himself. So, reluctantly, he turned away from the cupboard.

"Perhaps I'll look in the kitchen next," he decided. "There may be an eating sort of surprise in there."

In the kitchen, Bear tried the cupboards first.

"Pots and pans, bowls and plates, cups and saucers, but no surprises," he said sadly to himself.

He tried the fridge next.

"Butter and milk, yogurt and eggs, tomatoes and lettuce... Oh! And a huge cake covered in pink icing, with sugar teddies dancing round the side!"

Bear thought for a moment. "A special cake... Special cakes with pink icing mean special occasions, and special occasions mean surprises. So this *must* be a surprise!" he decided.

But Bear was puzzled. *What* is *the special occasion?* he wondered.

Bear thought and thought. "I give up," he said to himself at last. "I'd better look in the dining room next. There may be a clue in there."

Bear pushed open the door and looked around.

"Table and chairs, knives and forks, plates and glasses. No surprises here."

He looked again.

"Oh! And balloons and funny hats!"

Bear thought for a moment. "Balloons and funny hats mean parties," he told himself, "and parties mean special occasions, and special occasions mean surprises. But *what* is the special occasion?"

Bear sat down and thought even harder. *It can't be Christmas — I haven't seen a Christmas tree...*

He thought some more. *I wonder if it's... could it be...?* Suddenly Bear tingled with excitement.

"Yes! That's it!" he said, jumping up. "It must be... it's got to be... my birthday! And Sally and her mum want it to be a surprise for me!"

Bear smiled a big smile as he climbed the stairs. *I'd better go to bed now*, he thought. *Tomorrow is going to be a big day for me.*

Next afternoon, Bear watched as Sally put on her party dress and party shoes. He was bursting with anticipation.

My big moment, thought Bear as Sally carried him downstairs.

The dining room was full of children wearing the funny hats and playing with the balloons. Oh! And there on the table Bear could see the wrapped-up present. Next to it was the cake with the pink icing and the sugar teddies dancing round the side.

That's funny! thought Bear, as he counted the candles on the cake. *I didn't know I was five.*

At that moment, all the children started singing:

> "Happy birthday to you,
> Happy birthday to you."

Bear listened happily.

> "Happy birthday, dear Sally,
> Happy birthday to you!"

Bear couldn't believe his ears. It was *Sally's* birthday, not his. This was the wrong sort of surprise! It was awful.

All the children were laughing and shouting. Sally was smiling. Bear felt disappointed, sad and forgotten.

Then all at once Sally announced, "I'm going to blow out the candles. And my special friend Bear is going to help me." She tied the pink ribbon from the parcel in a big bow round his neck, and gave him a pink party hat.

Bear brightened up. He hadn't been forgotten after all!

Sally took a big breath. So did Bear. All five candles went out with one puff.

Or was it two?

"Happy birthday, Sally!" cried the children. "Well done, Bear!"

Bear grinned to himself. He felt very smart in his party hat and bow. And he felt proud to be Sally's special friend. It was a happy surprise after all.

The Bear at the Bus Stop

"Look, Dad," cried the girl. "Someone's left their teddy at the bus stop."

"So they have," said Dad. "Do you think we should take him home with us?"

"Oh no!" cried the girl. "What if his owner comes back and Teddy isn't here?"

Just then the bus came. And the girl and her dad disappeared.

Before the next bus came, a lady came along. She was on her way to a jumble sale.

"Wouldn't you look nice on my Book and Toy Stall!" she told Teddy. But then she thought again.

"I'm sure your owner will be here very soon," she said. "So here's one of my books to sit on, to make you more comfortable while you wait."

46

47

Before the next bus, a childminder arrived. The children she was looking after squealed and pointed. "I want that bear!" they cried together.

But the childminder was firm. "That bear belongs to someone else," she said. "But I'm sure he won't mind if we read his book while we wait."

The children enjoyed Teddy's book so much that they left him one of their chewy chocolate bars.

Before the next bus, three big boys came along.

"Hey," one of them cried. "Here's a bear we can chuck around on the bus!"

The biggest boy made a grab for Teddy. *Whoops!* Off came Teddy's arm.

"How was I supposed to know his arm was loose?" complained the biggest boy. And he delved into his pocket for his Wonder Knife.

Carefully and very gently, the biggest boy put Teddy back together. "Better than he was in the first place!" he beamed.

All day long the people who met Teddy wondered if he would be all right. When they got off the bus that evening, they couldn't wait to see if he was still there.

"Oh!" they all said in turn. "He's gone!"

But then they spotted a note:

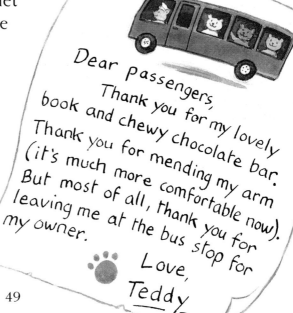

Dear passengers,
Thank you for my lovely book and chewy chocolate bar.
Thank you for mending my arm (it's much more comfortable now).
But most of all, thank you for leaving me at the bus stop for my owner.
Love,
Teddy

No Fun Fair for Freddy

Pippa and Freddy went almost everywhere together.

But Pippa was a girl who easily became excited and… forgetful!

"Where's Freddy?" Mum would say at bedtime. And then there would be a frantic search.

Freddy had been left everywhere, from the library to the swimming pool.

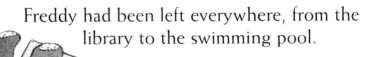

In the end, Mum made him a special badge. On it were his name, address and telephone number. And kind people were always either delivering Freddy to the door or telephoning for him to be collected.

One day, Pippa was particularly excited. A fun fair was coming to town the following week! But, right from the start, Mum was firm.

"No fun fair for Freddy," she announced. "It wouldn't be safe. It wouldn't be sensible. Freddy might get lost or squashed in no time at all."

All week Pippa argued. And the day before the fun fair, she decided to make a *huge* effort.

"If I show Mum that I can be really responsible," Pippa told herself, "then perhaps Freddy can come to the fun fair after all."

That afternoon, Pippa, Freddy and Mum set off for the shops. On the way, they delivered a parcel to Mike's mum.

"Come in," she said. "Mike's building a spaceship."

Pippa clutched Freddy firmly as she raced up the stairs.

"Oooh!" squealed Pippa, when she saw the kit. "Can I help?"

The two friends had a terrific time together. But just as Mum and Pippa were leaving, Mike's mum came running after them.

"Don't forget Freddy," she cried kindly, "or he might fly to the moon without you!"

Pippa blushed. Mum didn't say a word. But Pippa knew exactly what she was thinking: "No fun fair for Freddy!"

When they reached the supermarket, it was even busier than usual. While Mum pushed the trolley, Pippa gave all her attention to Freddy.

But just before the checkout there was a special display.

"Oooh!" squealed Pippa. "It's my favourite snack!" And she rushed forward to load the trolley.

Pippa and Mum chatted happily as they left the store. But suddenly the manager came running after them.

"Don't forget your teddy," he cried kindly, "or he might eat too many Crunchy Crisp-O-s!"

Mum didn't say a word. But Pippa muttered miserably, "No fun fair for Freddy!"

On the way home, Pippa, Freddy and Mum stopped off at the park.

Pippa pushed Freddy carefully on the swings. They whizzed down the slide in a bear hug.

But suddenly Pippa caught sight of Katie.

"Oooh!" squealed Pippa. "Do you want to play hide-and-seek with me?"

At last Mum and Pippa waved goodbye. But then a big boy came running after them.

"Hey!" he called. "Don't forget your bear, or he might get trampled in our game!"

When they got home, Pippa threw herself on her bed. "I don't want to go to the fun fair," she wailed. "Not without Freddy!"

All night long, Pippa tried not to think about the fun fair. But pictures of exciting rides and wonderful things to eat kept filling her dreams.

In the morning, Pippa rummaged on her tousled bed. "Where's Freddy?" she asked sleepily.

And then Pippa saw him.

Freddy was perched on the shelf, looking pleased with himself. He was smartly dressed… in Pippa's old baby sling!

"One of my better brain waves," said Mum, smiling proudly.

And, as soon as she had adjusted the straps to fit Pippa perfectly, Freddy was… all set for the fun fair!

My Bear

I'd like to be a pilot
And hurtle through the air,
But even if I looped the loop,
I still would need my bear.

I'd like to be a jockey
And ride a frisky mare,
But even if I won the race
I still would need my bear.

I'd like to be a gymnast
And dangle for a dare,
But even if I wowed the crowd,
I still would need my bear.

I'd like to be a pop star
With rings and purple hair,
But even if I made you scream,
I still would need my bear.

I'd like to be a teacher–
What lessons I'd prepare!
But even if I knew it all,
I still would need my bear.

It's fun to plan and daydream,
It's better still to share.
So even when he's old and worn,
I still will need my bear.

My Owner

My owner has a rumply bed;
She sometimes doesn't wash!
But even when she snores or squirms,
I never mind a squash.

"Let's play a game," she sometimes cries,
And, "Teddy, you begin."
But sometimes when we play a game,
I *wish* she'd let me win!

My owner sometimes stamps and shouts
(She's not a pretty sight!),
But even when the grown-ups glare,
I'm there to hold her tight.

My owner likes to go on trips
By boat or train or bus.
And if I didn't go as well,
I know there'd be a fuss.

We have our ups and downs of days,
But still we both agree,
I wouldn't change her for the world,
And nor would she change me.

Marcus and Lionel

Marcus and Lionel had been together for as long as they could remember. They lived on the little girl's bed, propped up against her pillow.

Marcus often went places with the little girl. And when he got home, he always told Lionel about his adventures. Lionel was too big to travel, and never got to go anywhere. Sometimes he wished he could have an adventure of his own, but most of the time he was content to sit on the bed and hear about the world outside.

One summer morning, there was lots of bustle and clatter in the house. People had come with boxes for packing things, and there was a van to take everything away. The little girl and her parents were moving to the countryside.

Marcus was going to ride in the car. But Lionel was packed in a box, along with the pillows and some blankets. He just had time to say goodbye to Marcus before the lid was shut.

Marcus had a wonderful journey. There was so much to see! They rode through busy city streets, one after the other.

Then they came to a big bridge. Marcus had never seen a bridge before. *Wait until I tell Lionel about this!* he thought.

As they crossed the bridge, Marcus saw boats in the water. When they got to the other side, he saw hills and a windmill and cows in fields.

I can't wait to tell Lionel! he thought.

At last they arrived at the new house. There were trees at the front, and swings and a slide at the back. The little girl's bedroom looked out over a garden with red roses growing in it.

Lionel and I will be happy here, Marcus thought.

The little girl and her parents started to unpack the boxes. Marcus could hardly wait to see Lionel.

They unpacked the little girl's clothes, and all her books. They unpacked her doll's house and her cowboy hat and boots. There was no sign of Lionel yet.

They unpacked the tea set, the easel and the bedside lamp. There was still no sign of Lionel.

There was only one box left. *Lionel* has *to be in that one,* Marcus thought.

But he wasn't. It was only the little girl's games and jigsaws.

That night, the little girl had to sleep with her mother's pillow – and no Lionel. She hugged Marcus extra tight, and Marcus tried hard to hug her back.

"I'm sure Lionel will turn up," he thought. But Lionel didn't.

Over the next few days, Marcus and the little girl had lots of new things to explore. There were trees to climb, and a little stream with frogs and fish. There was a hidey-hole in one of the big trees, and there were four cats next door who came to visit.

Discovering it all should have been a great adventure for Marcus, but it wasn't much fun. Lionel wasn't there to hear about it when Marcus came home.

The days seemed very long.

One day, the little girl took Marcus out to the car. She and her mum were going to visit someone in the city, and Marcus was going, too.

On the way, Marcus saw lots of things he remembered from the moving day. That made him miss Lionel more than ever.

When they got to the city, the little girl carried Marcus in her usual way – by one arm. This always gave Marcus an interesting view of things.

And that day Marcus got a *very* interesting view of something. Behind an iron gate, on the lawn in front of a big grey building, there were tables with all sorts of things set out on display: chairs and clothes and clocks and books...

And right there, on one of those tables, was… could it be?

Yes! It was… Lionel!

Marcus had to make the little girl stop, so she would see Lionel, too. But how? She and her mum seemed to be in such a hurry!

There was only one way. Gathering all his strength, Marcus stuck out one leg — just far enough to get his foot caught in the gate.

As the little girl walked on, Marcus's foot began to tear. It hurt terribly. But it would be worth it, if only…

"Mum, wait," said the little girl, stopping. "Marcus's foot is stuck."

As the little girl began to free his foot, she suddenly saw what Marcus had seen.

"Mum!" she cried. "Mum, look! It's Lionel! We found him, Mum! We found Lionel!"

Indeed they had. He was a bit dusty, and one of his seams was torn, but otherwise he was fine. They got him from the jumble sale, and that afternoon they took him home to the countryside.

The little girl's mum mended his seam and gave him a bath. She mended Marcus's foot, too, so it didn't hurt any more.

Marcus and Lionel were so happy to be together again. They spent days and days catching up on all that had happened. It was just like old times.

Well, almost: now Lionel had some adventures to tell Marcus about, too!

Edward's First Party

Edward stood on his head. Next he turned a cartwheel. Then he simply sat on his bed and squirmed.

Tomorrow Edward was going to his first Teddy Bear Party.

Fabulous food! Great games! And lots of new bears to meet! he thought to himself.

But then Edward gave a little frown. Because Edward's owner, Tina, had been invited, too. And Tina had *terrible* table manners.

Edward began to fret.

"What if Tina rushes at her food? What if she chatters with her mouth full? And what if… oh no!…" Edward blushed at the thought. *What if Tina gets her horrible hiccups?*

Next morning Edward woke up feeling excited and anxious all at once.

Tina was excited, too. At breakfast she told Dad all about the party. And, although she ate an egg, toast, cereal and orange juice, she didn't stop talking once.

At lunch Tina lunged for the sauce. Then she gobbled down her meal and rushed upstairs to choose her party clothes.

Then Edward heard her, all the way from downstairs.

"Hic-hic! Hic-hic!"

"Oh no!" groaned Edward. "There she goes!"

Mum made Tina drink a glass of water upside down. Then Mum, Tina and Edward walked very gently to the party. Edward kept his paws crossed all the way.

But just as Mum rang the doorbell – "Hic!" – Tina got hiccups again. Edward didn't know where to put himself.

At last the door opened. Edward was almost too embarrassed to go inside. But when he did, Edward couldn't believe his eyes – or his ears!

Because all the bear owners were rushing at their food. They all seemed to be shrieking as they ate. And, to Edward's delight, every single owner had… hiccups!

71

Whizz Fizz Bear

Nigel liked a night-time nibble. As soon as the house was quiet, he would creep downstairs to explore the fridge.

Nigel's favourite food was cheese. And one day Nigel's owner, Harry, popped something really tasty into the shopping trolley.

"Good heavens, Harry!" cried Dad. "This cheese is *exceptional!*"

Nigel waited impatiently for night-time. At last the house was quiet.

"Mmmm!" murmured Nigel as he sampled the latest flavour. And before he knew it, Nigel's nibble had become a mammoth meal.

Now Nigel was feeling thirsty... *very* thirsty. He delved deeper into the fridge.

"Bother!" grumbled Nigel. "This carton of orange juice is empty." But then he saw the bottle.

FUN FIZZ said the cheerful label. And then, in smaller letters, *'guaranteed to quench your thirst'*.

Nigel reached for it eagerly. He'd never managed to open a bottle by himself before. But this time he was in luck – the bottle was half empty, and the cap was loose.

Whizz, Fizz! A million bubbles tickled Nigel's nose.

Whizz, Fizz! Nigel had never tasted *anything* like it!

Very soon the bottle was empty.

But then Nigel noticed the crate. It was parked by the back door, and it was *full* of Fizz.

Nigel skipped across the kitchen. But this time he was out of luck. Because, though he tried every single bottle, he couldn't open any of them.

Reluctantly, Nigel padded back to bed. But he couldn't get the Fizz out of his mind.

Nigel tossed and turned. He'd never been so thirsty. Then, suddenly, he found himself back in the quiet kitchen again. And this time it was a different story.

"Whizz, Fizz, wow!" cried Nigel, as he opened the first bottle with ease. "Being thirsty must have made me stronger!

Whizz, Fizz! Whizz, Fizz! Nigel worked his way steadily through the crate. By the time he reached the last bottle, he was feeling light-headed, light-pawed and...

"Help!" cried Nigel. He was so full of bubbles that he had begun to float – just like a helium balloon!

First Nigel glided through the kitchen. Next he hovered in the hall. Then – *whoosh!* – he floated up the stairs and into Harry's bedroom.

"Oh no!" cried Nigel. "The window's open!"

74

Nigel was in a panic. He didn't want to fly off into the night. He would be heartbroken to leave his happy home and fridge.

So, with a desperate lunge, Nigel grabbed hold of Harry's bookshelf.

Crash! Down came all Harry's books. And so did Nigel.

Slowly, he opened one eye. But all Nigel could see was the familiar design on Harry's wallpaper.

Gradually, Nigel came to his senses. Then, suddenly, he gave a great "Whoop!"

"I didn't drink all the Fizz after all!" cried Nigel. "I've just been having a nightmare, and I've fallen out of bed."

Nigel wriggled with relief. But he was still thirsty. Then he saw the tumbler of water. Harry's dad had left it by the bed, just in case the new cheese had made Harry thirsty. Nigel drank deeply. Then he settled back into bed and a happy, dreamlike sleep.

The next day Harry's family had visitors. Harry and Nigel were on their best behaviour.

And, when the drinks were poured, Nigel shook his head politely at the Fizz.

"No thanks," he seemed to say. "Mine's an orange juice."

The Bear and the Babysitter

The new babysitter was due any minute. And Buster was sulking in Ben's room.

The last babysitter had been bossy and banished them to bed early. The babysitter before that had been fussy. *She'd* scrubbed behind their ears!

And now… *ding, dong!*

Help! Here she is! thought Buster. And he slid smartly into Ben's playhouse.

Buster could hear hello and goodbye noises coming from the hall.
Then he heard Ben calling his name.

But, although Buster sat in the playhouse for a long time, there
were no getting-ready-for-bed noises. And once or twice he
thought he heard squeaks of excitement.

Buster padded softly onto the landing and listened again.

"Oh no!" he groaned. "They're playing my favourite game. And they've started without me!"

Buster squirmed with disappointment.

Then – *Brring! Brring!* – the phone rang in the kitchen.

Whoosh! As soon as the babysitter left the living room, Buster whizzed down the stairs.

"A wrong number," the babysitter explained, coming back into the hall. Then she caught sight of Buster at the bottom of the stairs, looking innocent and interesting.

"Look, Ben!" she cried. "I told you your teddy would turn up. Now he can join in our game."

Buster and Ben went to bed late that evening. There was barely time to wash before their story. And, when she tucked them in, the babysitter smiled kindly.

"The first family I babysat for," she confided, "were a bit bossy. And the next family were fairly fussy. But this must be third time lucky," she said, "because you two are *brilliant!*"

And so are you, thought Buster. *And so are you.*

The Teddy
Who Wanted a T-shirt

Sandy looked in the mirror in disgust.

"Same old velvet waistcoat. Boring old spotty tie," he grumbled. "I must be the worst-dressed bear in town."

Later that day, Sandy's owner had a visitor. And Tess had brought *her* teddy.

When they were introduced, Sandy wriggled in his wretched waistcoat. He squirmed in his terrible tie. Because the visiting teddy looked terrific… in a trendy new T-shirt.

That evening Sandy stuffed his tie down the side of the chair. He turned his waistcoat back to front.

"But it still doesn't look like a T-shirt," he growled.

The next day, Sandy's owner went shopping. He came home with a carrier bag full of new T-shirts.

Mum suddenly got brisk and busy. "We'll pass on all your outgrown T-shirts," she announced. "But first we must give them a wash."

Sandy's owner parked him on the washing machine and ran out to play.

Sandy looked on with longing as Mum loaded in the T-shirts. "Ooooh, look at those lovely stripes!" he sighed.

No sooner had Mum disappeared than Sandy shuffled to the front of the machine. Gingerly, he leaned over the edge to look for the STOP button.

If only I could rescue just one T-shirt, he thought to himself. But everything looked so strange upside down. And, instead of the STOP button, Sandy's nose nudged the EXTRA HOT button.

Later, when Mum unloaded the machine, she squealed in surprise. Because every single T-shirt had been shrunk… to *exactly* Sandy's size!

85

Midnight in the Park

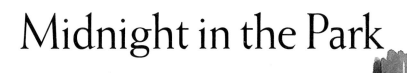

You know the bear from Number Nine,
She likes to play at night.
Down the drainpipe watch her whizz,
There's not a soul in sight.

She tries a cartwheel on the grass,
She longs to stretch her paws.
Then on the swing she starts to sing,
"It's great to be outdoors!"

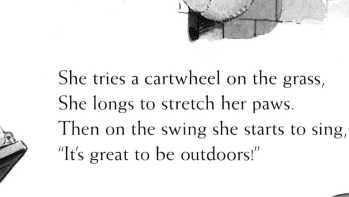

"Psst!" Someone's creeping up the path,
They want to try the slide.
It's Twenty-three and Seven B:
"We couldn't stay inside!"

Now Twenty-two is coming too,
And Seventeen and Four,
They're jumping off the climbing frame,
Then running back for more.

But suddenly a light appears,
"What's going on out there?"
A small boy cries and tries to see,
"And where's my teddy bear?"

Up the drainpipe, home they go,
Before it starts to rain,
They leave the park all still and dark,
But they'll be back again!

Christmas Bear

A tear rolled down Sally's cheek as her mother switched off the bedroom light. It was Christmas Eve, and Sally had forgotten to post her letter to Santa Claus. She had found it stuffed in her jacket pocket.

How would Santa know what Sally really wanted? Maybe he'd forget her altogether!

Sally and her parents had still put out two mince pies and a glass of milk to welcome Santa. The red stocking hung ready at the foot of her bed as it did every Christmas Eve. But this year Sally was sure it would remain empty.

She sniffed miserably to herself as she drifted off to sleep…

Meanwhile, a bright shape was racing through the starry sky. It was Santa Claus, riding in his biggest sleigh, pulled by his fastest reindeer!

The sleigh was filled with sacks of presents, neatly sorted and labelled for children all over the world.

But in one of the sacks something was stirring...

A little paw appeared, and then another. Then two ears, followed by a furry head and a furry body.

It was a teddy bear... a very naughty teddy bear!

The sleigh made a sudden turn. One second the teddy bear was safe inside the sack, and the next he was tumbling down, over and over and over. He gave one shrill squeak, but Santa Claus heard nothing except the rushing of the wind and the jingling of the reindeer's bells.

Over and over Bear fell, towards white fields far below.
  Down…
      and down…
          and down he went…
until suddenly he landed in the snow-laden branches of a fir tree.

"Ouch!" he cried as he slid through the prickly branches and disappeared into a deep snowdrift.

All was still and silent and very, very cold.

Bear couldn't tell whether he was upside down or the right way up. It was some time before he pushed away the snow and found himself looking out into the night.

A little way off he saw a person dressed all in white.

"Aha!" said Bear. *"There's* someone who will help me."

He struggled to his feet and trudged through the snow, which as you can imagine seemed very deep to a little bear.

"Excuse me," he called out as he came closer. "Can you please tell me where I am?"

There was no answer from the person dressed in white.

Bear tried once more. "Excuse me," he said loudly. "Can you tell me where I am?"

Again there was no answer. The person in white didn't even look down to see who was talking.

"Well!" said Bear, turning away. "I hope all the people here aren't so rude!"

Bear was now feeling very cold and sorry for himself. He wished he was safe and snug in Santa's sack.

He sighed and looked around. Not far off there was a house. *And where there is a house,* Bear thought to himself, *there will be people and warmth.*

He walked round the house twice, trying to find a way in, but the door handles and windows were all too high for him to reach.

He was about to give up when a black cat came padding round the corner. It stopped and looked the little bear up and down, its fur bristling and its whiskers twitching. Then, deciding that bears were of no great interest, the cat turned and walked away.

The cat climbed up some steps to a closed door and then vanished completely. The last Bear saw of it was its tail disappearing through the unopened door.

A magic cat! thought Bear.

But he soon discovered that the cat had its own private cat-sized door. There in front of him was a hinged flap.

Bear reached up and pushed himself against it. The next thing he knew, he was tumbling head-first through the opening.

Bear thumped down onto a soft carpet. What bliss to be inside!

For a minute he lay still with his eyes shut, enjoying the warmth and comfort. Then he opened his eyes.

It was very dark. In front of him there was a staircase, and at the top he saw a dim light.

It's time for a good snooze, Bear thought. He'd had enough adventures for a while.

Bear dragged himself up towards the light. He was out of breath when he pulled himself up the last step.

The light was coming from an open door. From inside, Bear could hear the sound of soft breathing.

He tiptoed to the door and nearly tripped over something lying just inside. It was a plate with two mince pies on it! Next to it was a small glass of milk.

Now, Bear felt very hungry indeed. He sat himself down by the plate and ate steadily and happily until he had finished both pies.

How kind of them to think of me! Bear thought, gulping down the milk.

It was only then that he started to look around the room. In one corner there was a bed, and in it someone was sleeping peacefully.

"That's where I'd like to be," Bear whispered.

It wasn't easy getting up onto the bed, but he finally did it. A tired bear can be a very determined bear if he spots a comfortable place to sleep.

The effort was worth it. For what should he find at the end of the bed but a cosy red sleeping bag. It was just the right size!

In no time at all, he snuggled his way into it and fell fast asleep...

Sally opened her eyes. It was morning. *Christmas* morning!

But Sally's heart sank as she remembered her unposted letter to Santa.

Had he brought her anything at all? She looked towards the door. The mince pies and the milk had gone!

Quickly she crawled down to the bottom of the bed. The red stocking was no longer flat and empty. It was bulging. There really *was* something in it!

Bursting with excitement, she reached in and pulled out… a furry teddy bear!

Sally gazed at it wide-eyed. "But how could Santa have known you were exactly what I wanted?" she asked the little bear, thinking of the letter in her jacket pocket. This is what it said:

Dear Santa,
   Please can I have my very own bear for Christmas?

Lots of love
Sally
xxx

Was it Sally's imagination, or did the little bear seem to smile?

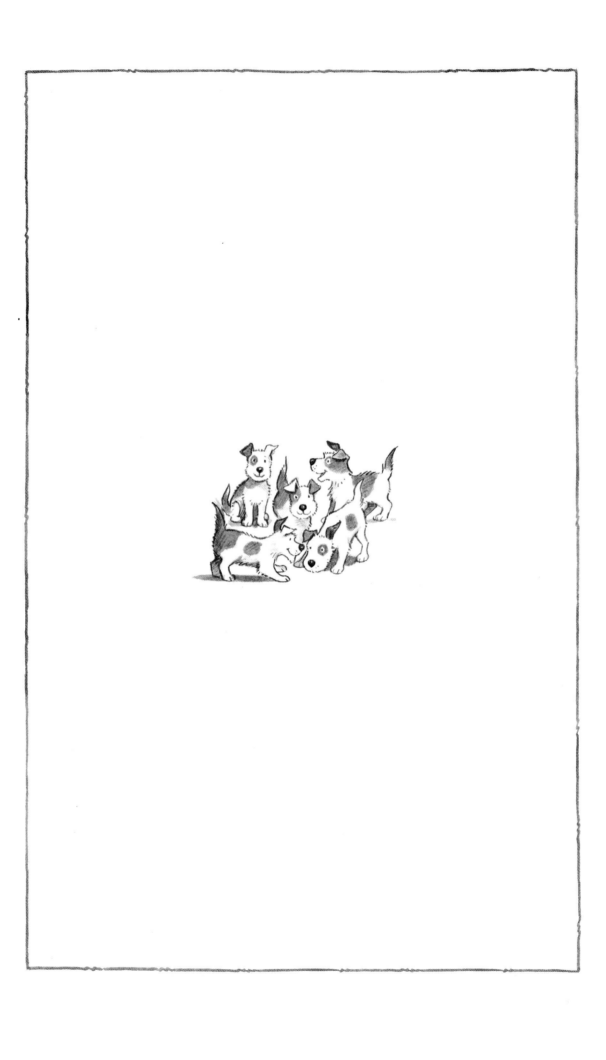

NURSERY RHYMES

About the nursery rhymes...

Nursery rhymes are part of growing up. Children of all ages love to listen to, join in with, and repeat rhymes. This collection brings together more than one hundred and fifty rhymes, grouped into four sections, featuring favourites like *Humpty Dumpty*, playtime rhymes like *I'm a Little Teapot*, number rhymes like *One, Two, Buckle My Shoe* and bedtime rhymes like *Rock-a-bye Baby*.

Contents

Goosey, Goosey, Gander

Goosey, goosey, gander,
　　Whither shall I wander?
Upstairs, downstairs,
　　In my lady's chamber.
There I met an old man
　　Who would not say his prayers.
I took him by the left leg
　　And threw him down the stairs.

Jack and Jill

Jack and Jill went up the hill
To fetch a pail of water.
Jack fell down and broke his crown,
And Jill came tumbling after.

Up Jack got, and home did trot,
As fast as he could caper,
To old Dame Dob, who patched his nob
With vinegar and brown paper.

Mary Had a Little Lamb

Mary had a little lamb,
Its fleece was white as snow,
And everywhere that Mary went
The lamb was sure to go.

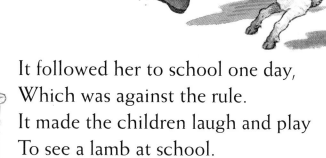

It followed her to school one day,
Which was against the rule.
It made the children laugh and play
To see a lamb at school.

And so the teacher turned it out,
But still it lingered near,
And waited patiently about
Till Mary did appear.

"What makes the lamb love Mary so?"
The eager children cry.
"Why, Mary loves the lamb, you know,"
The teacher did reply.

Baa, Baa, Black Sheep

Baa, baa, black sheep, have you any wool?
Yes, sir, yes, sir, three bags full.
One for the master, and one for the dame,
And one for the little boy who lives in the lane.

Little Boy Blue

Little Boy Blue, come blow your horn!
The sheep's in the meadow, the cow's in the corn.
Where is the boy who looks after the sheep?
He's under the haycock, fast asleep.
Will you wake him? No, not I!
For if I do, he's sure to cry.

Little Bo-peep

Little Bo-peep has lost her sheep,
And doesn't know where to find them.
Leave them alone, and they'll come home,
Bringing their tails behind them.

Little Bo-peep fell fast asleep,
And dreamt she heard them bleating.
But when she awoke, she found it a joke,
For they were still a-fleeting.

Then up she took her little crook,
Determined for to find them.
She found them indeed, but it made her heart bleed,
For they'd left their tails behind them.

Little Bird

Once I saw a little bird
Come hop, hop, hop.
So I cried, "Little bird,
Will you stop, stop, stop?"

I was going to the window
To say, "How do you do?"
But he shook his little tail,
And far away he flew.

Summer Breeze

Summer breeze, so softly blowing,
In my garden pinks are growing.
If you go and send the showers,
You may come and smell my flowers.

Mary, Mary

Mary, Mary, quite contrary,
How does your garden grow?
With silver bells and cockle shells,
And pretty maids all in a row!

Grey Goose and Gander

Grey goose and gander,
 Waft your wings together,
And carry the good King's daughter
 Over the one-strand river.

I Had a Little Nut Tree

I had a little nut tree,
 Nothing would it bear
But a silver nutmeg
 And a golden pear.

The King of Spain's daughter
 Came to visit me,
And all for the sake
 Of my little nut tree.

111

Bobby Shaftoe

Bobby Shaftoe's gone to sea,
Silver buckles on his knee.
He'll come back and marry me,
Bonny Bobby Shaftoe!

Bobby Shaftoe's fat and fair,
Combing down his yellow hair.
He's my love forevermore,
Bonny Bobby Shaftoe!

Rub-a-Dub-Dub

Rub-a-dub-dub,
Three men in a tub,
And how do you think they got there?
The butcher, the baker,
The candlestick-maker,
They all jumped out of a rotten potato,
'Twas enough to make a man stare.

I Saw a Ship A-Sailing

I saw a ship a-sailing,
    A-sailing on the sea,
And oh, but it was laden
    With pretty things for thee.

There were comfits in the cabin,
    And apples in the hold.
The sails were made of silk,
    And the masts were made of gold.

The four-and-twenty sailors
    That stood between the decks
Were four and twenty white mice
    With chains about their necks.

The captain was a duck
    With a packet on his back,
And when the ship began to move,
    The captain said, "Quack! Quack!"

Old King Cole

Old King Cole was a merry old soul,
And a merry old soul was he.
He called for his pipe, and he called for his bowl,
And he called for his fiddlers three.

Each fiddler he had a fiddle,
And the fiddles went tweedle-dee.
Oh, there's none so rare as can compare
With King Cole and his fiddlers three.

Sing a Song of Sixpence

Sing a song of sixpence,
A pocket full of rye.
Four and twenty blackbirds
Baked in a pie.

When the pie was opened,
The birds began to sing.
Wasn't that a dainty dish
To set before the King?

The King was in the counting house,
Counting out his money.
The Queen was in the parlour,
Eating bread and honey.

The maid was in the garden,
Hanging out the clothes,
When down came a blackbird
And pecked off her nose!

Little Miss Muffet

Little Miss Muffet
Sat on a tuffet,
Eating her curds and whey.
There came a big spider,
Who sat down beside her,
And frightened Miss Muffet away.

Curly Locks

Curly Locks, Curly Locks, wilt thou be mine?
Thou shalt not wash dishes, nor yet feed the swine,
But sit on a cushion and sew a fine seam,
And feast upon strawberries, sugar and cream.

Little Tommy Tucker

Little Tommy Tucker
Sings for his supper.
What shall he eat?
White bread and butter.

How will he cut it
Without e'er a knife?
How will he marry
Without e'er a wife?

Little Jack Horner

Little Jack Horner sat in a corner,
Eating his Christmas pie.
He put in his thumb,
And pulled out a plum,
And said, "What a good boy am I!"

Little Betty Blue

Little Betty Blue
Lost her holiday shoe.
What can little Betty do?
Give her another,
To match the other,
And then she may walk in two.

The Queen of Hearts

The Queen of Hearts,
She made some tarts,
All on a summer's day.
The Knave of Hearts,
He stole the tarts,
And took them clean away.

The King of Hearts
Called for the tarts,
And beat the Knave full sore.
The Knave of Hearts
Brought back the tarts,
And vowed he'd steal no more.

The Lion and the Unicorn

The Lion and the Unicorn
Were fighting for the crown.
The Lion beat the Unicorn
All around the town.
Some gave them white bread,
Some gave them brown,
Some gave them plum cake,
And drummed them out of town.

Humpty Dumpty

Humpty Dumpty sat on a wall,
Humpty Dumpty had a great fall.
    All the King's horses
    And all the King's men
Couldn't put Humpty together again.

Ride a Cockhorse

Ride a cockhorse to Banbury Cross,
To see a fine lady upon a white horse.
Rings on her fingers and bells on her toes,
And she shall have music wherever she goes.

Hickory, Dickory, Dock

Hickory, dickory, dock,
The mouse ran up the clock.
The clock struck one,
The mouse ran down.
Hickory, dickory, dock!

Pussy Cat, Pussy Cat

Pussy cat, pussy cat, where have you been?
"I've been to London to visit the Queen."
Pussy cat, pussy cat, what did you there?
"I frightened a little mouse under the chair."

Six Little Mice

Six little mice sat down to spin,
Pussy passed by, and she peeped in.
What are you doing, my little men?
"We're weaving shirts for gentlemen."
Can I come in and cut off your threads?
"No, no, Mistress Pussy, you'd cut off our heads!"

I Love Little Pussy

I love little pussy, her coat is so warm,
And if I don't hurt her, she'll do me no harm.
So I'll not pull her tail, nor drive her away,
But pussy and I very gently will play.

Jack Sprat

Jack Sprat could eat no fat,
His wife could eat no lean,
And so between them both,
They licked the platter clean.

Jack ate all the lean,
Joan ate all the fat.
The bone they picked clean,
Then gave it to the cat.

Old Mother Hubbard

Old Mother Hubbard
Went to the cupboard
To fetch her poor dog a bone.
But when she got there
The cupboard was bare,
And so the poor dog had none.

There Was an Old Woman

There was an old woman tossed up in a blanket,
    Seventeen times as high as the moon.
But where she was going no mortal could tell,
    For under her arm she carried a broom.
"Old woman, old woman, old woman," said I,
    "Whither, oh whither, oh whither so high?"
"To sweep the cobwebs from the sky,
    And I'll be with you by and by!"

Hey, Diddle, Diddle

Hey, diddle, diddle,
The cat and the fiddle,
The cow jumped over the moon.
The little dog laughed
To see such sport,
And the dish ran away with the spoon!

The Man in the Moon
Came Tumbling Down

The man in the moon came tumbling down,
And asked the way to Norwich.
He went by south, and burnt his mouth
With supping cold pease porridge.

Pease Porridge Hot

Pease porridge hot,
Pease porridge cold,
Pease porridge in the pot,
Nine days old.

Some like it hot,
Some like it cold,
Some like it in the pot,
Nine days old.

One Misty, Moisty Morning

One misty, moisty morning,
When cloudy was the weather,
I met with an old man
Clothed all in leather,
Clothed all in leather,
With cap under his chin.
"How do you?" and "How do you do?"
And "How do you do?" again.

Doctor Foster

Doctor Foster went to Gloucester
        In a shower of rain.
He stepped in a puddle, right up to his middle,
        And never went there again.

The Old Woman Who Lived in a Shoe

There was an old woman who lived in a shoe,
She had so many children she didn't know what to do.
She gave them some broth without any bread,
Then scolded them soundly and sent them to bed.

Peter, Peter, Pumpkin Eater

Peter, Peter, pumpkin eater,
Had a wife and couldn't keep her.
He put her in a pumpkin shell,
And there he kept her very well.

Peter, Peter, pumpkin eater,
Had another, and didn't love her.
Peter learned to read and spell,
And then he loved her very well.

Georgie Porgie

Georgie Porgie, pudding and pie,
Kissed the girls and made them cry.
When the boys came out to play,
Georgie Porgie ran away.

Tweedledum and Tweedledee

Tweedledum and Tweedledee
    Agreed to fight a battle,
For Tweedledum said Tweedledee
    Had spoilt his nice new rattle.
Just then flew by a monstrous crow
    As big as a tar barrel,
Which frightened both the heroes so,
    They quite forgot their quarrel.

How Many Days?

How many days has my baby to play?
Saturday, Sunday, Monday,
Tuesday, Wednesday, Thursday, Friday,
Saturday, Sunday, Monday.
Hop away, skip away,
My baby wants to play,
My baby wants to play every day!

Dance to Your Daddy

Dance to your daddy,
My little babby,
Dance to your daddy,
My little lamb!

You shall have a fishy
In a little dishy,
You shall have a fishy
When the boat comes in!

Catch Him, Crow

Catch him, crow! Carry him, kite!
Take him away till the apples are ripe.
When they are ripe and ready to fall,
Here comes baby, apples and all!

Up, Up, Up

Here we go up, up, up.
And here we go down, down, down.
Here we go backwards and forwards,
And here we go round and round!

Dance, Little Baby

Dance, little baby, dance up high!
Never mind, baby, Mother is by.
Crow and caper, caper and crow,
There, little baby, there you go.
Up to the ceiling, down to the ground,
Backwards and forwards, round and round!
Dance little baby, and Mother shall sing,
With the merry chorus, ding-a-ding, ding.

Clap, Clap Handies

Clap, clap handies,
Mummy's wee one.
Clap, clap handies,
Till Daddy comes home,
Home to his bonny wee baby.
Clap, clap handies,
My bonny wee one.

Pat-a-Cake

Pat-a-cake, pat-a-cake, baker's man!
Bake me a cake as fast as you can.
Roll it and pat it and mark it with "B",
And put it in the oven for baby and me.

Five Little Mice

This little mousie peeped within,
This little mousie walked right in!
This little mousie came to play,
This little mousie ran away!
This little mousie cried, "Dear me!
Dinner is done and it's time for tea!"

Two Little Dickey Birds

Two little dickey birds sat upon a hill,
One named Jack, the other named Jill.
Fly away, Jack! Fly away, Jill!
Come again, Jack! Come again, Jill!

Dance, Thumbkin, Dance

Dance, Thumbkin, dance,
Dance, ye merry men, every one.
But Thumbkin, he can dance alone,
Thumbkin, he can dance alone.

Dance, Foreman, dance,
Dance, ye merry men, every one.
But Foreman, he can dance alone,
Foreman, he can dance alone.

Dance, Longman, dance,
Dance, ye merry men, every one,
But Longman, he can dance alone,
Longman, he can dance alone.

Dance, Ringman, dance,
Dance, ye merry men, every one,
But Ringman, he can dance alone,
Ringman, he can dance alone.

Dance, Littleman, dance,
Dance, ye merry men, every one.
But Littleman, he can dance alone,
Littleman, he can dance alone.

Incy Wincy Spider

Incy Wincy Spider climbed up the water spout.
Down came the rain and washed the spider out.
Out came the sunshine, dried up all the rain,
And Incy Wincy Spider climbed up the spout again.

Here Sits the Lord Mayor

Here sits the Lord Mayor,
Here sit two men.
Here sits the cock, and here sits the hen.
Here sit the little chickens,
And here they run in,
Chin-chopper,
Chin-chopper,
Chin-chopper, chin!

Round and Round the Garden

Round and round the garden,
Like a teddy bear.
One step, two steps,
Tickle you under there!

Teddy Bear, Teddy Bear

Teddy bear, teddy bear,
Turn around.
Teddy bear, teddy bear,
Touch the ground.

Teddy bear, teddy bear,
Climb the stairs.
Teddy bear, teddy bear,
Say your prayers.

Teddy bear, teddy bear,
Turn out the light.
Teddy bear, teddy bear,
Say good night.

Jack Be Nimble

Jack be nimble,
Jack be quick.
Jack jump over
The candlestick.

Jumping Joan

Here am I,
Little jumping Joan.
When nobody's with me,
I'm all alone.

Leg Over Leg

Leg over leg,
As the dog went to Dover.
When he came to a stile,
Hop! He went over.

Hogs in the Garden

Hogs in the garden, catch 'em, Towser.
Cows in the cornfield, run, boys, run.
Cats in the cream pot, run, girls, run.
Fire on the mountains, run, boys, run!

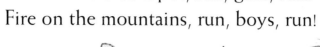

See-Saw, Margery Daw

See-saw, Margery Daw,
Jacky shall have a new master.
Jacky shall have but a penny a day,
Because he can't work any faster.

See-Saw, Sacra Down

See-saw, sacra down,
Which is the way to Boston town?
One foot up, the other foot down,
That is the way to Boston town.

This Is the Way the Ladies Ride

This is the way the ladies ride,
Nimble, nimble, nimble, nimble.
This is the way the gentlemen ride,
A gallop, a trot, a gallop, a trot.
This is the way the farmers ride,
Jiggety-jog, jiggety-jog.
And when they come to a hedge – they jump over!
And when they come to a slippery space –
They scramble, scramble, scramble,
Tumble-down Dick!

The Coachman

Up at Piccadilly, oh!
The coachman takes his stand,
And when he meets a pretty girl,
He takes her by the hand.
Whip away for ever, oh!
Drive away so clever, oh!
All the way to Bristol, oh!
He drives her four-in-hand.

Ride, Baby, Ride

Ride, baby, ride,
Pretty baby shall ride,
And have a little puppy dog tied to his side,
And a little pussy cat tied to the other,
And away he shall ride to see his grandmother,
To see his grandmother,
To see his grandmother.

You Ride Behind

You ride behind and I'll ride before,
And trot, trot away to Baltimore.
You shall take bread, and I will take honey,
And both of us carry a purse full of money.

To Market

To market, to market, to buy a fat pig,
Home again, home again, jiggety-jig.
To market, to market, to buy a fat hog,
Home again, home again, jiggety-jog.

This Little Pig

This little pig went to market,
This little pig stayed at home.
This little pig had roast beef,
This little pig had none.
And this little pig cried, "Wee-wee-wee,"
All the way home.

The Blacksmith

"Robert Barnes, my fellow fine,
Can you shoe this horse of mine?"
"Yes, indeed, that I can,
As well as any other man.
There's a nail, and there's a prod,
And now, you see, your horse is shod!"

Cobbler, Cobbler

Cobbler, cobbler, mend my shoe,
Get it done by half-past two.
Do it neat, and do it strong,
And I will pay you when it's done.

I'm a Little Teapot

I'm a little teapot,
Short and stout,
Here is my handle,
Here is my spout.
When I see the teacups,
Hear me shout,
"Tip me over and pour me out!"

Polly Put the Kettle On

Polly put the kettle on,
Polly put the kettle on,
Polly put the kettle on,
        We'll all have tea.

Sukey take it off again,
Sukey take it off again,
Sukey take it off again,
        They've all gone away.

Blow the fire and make the toast,
Put the muffins down to roast,
Blow the fire and make the toast,
        We'll all have tea.

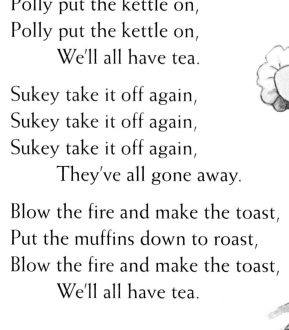

Wash the Dishes

Wash the dishes, wipe the dishes,
Ring the bell for tea.
Three good wishes, three good kisses,
I will give to thee.

Handy Pandy

Handy Pandy, Jack-a-dandy,
Loves plum cake and sugar candy.
He bought some at the grocer's shop,
And out he came, hop, hop, hop!

Girls and Boys, Come Out to Play

Girls and boys, come out to play,
The moon is shining bright as day.
Leave your supper and leave your sleep,
And come with your playfellows into the street.
Come with a whoop, and come with a call,
Come with a good will, or come not at all.
Come, let us dance on the open green,
And she who holds longest shall be our queen.

Round About the Rosebush

Round about the rosebush,
    Three steps,
    Four steps,
All the little boys and girls
    Are sitting
    On the doorsteps.

Ring-a-Ring o' Roses

Ring-a-ring o' roses,
A pocket full of posies.
A-tishoo! A-tishoo!
We all fall down!

Here We Go Round the Mulberry Bush

Here we go round the mulberry bush,
    The mulberry bush, the mulberry bush.
Here we go round the mulberry bush,
    On a cold and frosty morning.

This is the way we wash our clothes,
    Wash our clothes, wash our clothes.
This is the way we wash our clothes,
    On a cold and frosty morning.

Pop Goes the Weasel!

Up and down the City Road,
    In and out the Eagle,
That's the way the money goes,
    Pop goes the weasel!

Half a pound of tuppenny rice,
    Half a pound of treacle,
Mix it up and make it nice,
    Pop goes the weasel!

Bangalorey Man

Follow my Bangalorey Man,
Follow my Bangalorey Man,
I'll do all that ever I can
To follow my Bangalorey Man.

We'll borrow a horse and steal a gig,
And round the world we'll do a jig,
And I'll do all that ever I can
To follow my Bangalorey Man.

The Muffin Man

Oh, do you know the muffin man,
    The muffin man, the muffin man.
Oh, do you know the muffin man
    That lives in Drury Lane?

Oh, yes, I know the muffin man,
    The muffin man, the muffin man.
Oh, yes, I know the muffin man
    That lives in Drury Lane.

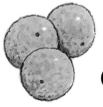

Oranges and Lemons

Oranges and lemons,
Say the bells of St Clement's.

You owe me five farthings,
Say the bells of St Martin's.

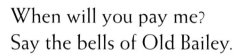

When will you pay me?
Say the bells of Old Bailey.

When I grow rich,
Say the bells at Shoreditch.

Pray, when will that be?
Say the bells of Stepney.

I'm sure I don't know,
Says the great bell at Bow.

Here comes a candle to light you to bed,
And here comes a chopper to chop off your head.

London Bridge

London Bridge is falling down,
  Falling down, falling down.
London Bridge is falling down,
  My fair lady.

Build it up with iron bars,
  Iron bars, iron bars.
Build it up with iron bars,
  My fair lady.

Iron bars will bend and break,
  Bend and break, bend and break.
Iron bars will bend and break,
  My fair lady.

Build it up with gold and silver,
  Gold and silver, gold and silver.
Build it up with gold and silver,
  My fair lady.

Gold and silver I've not got,
  I've not got, I've not got.
Gold and silver I've not got,
  My fair lady.

Then off to prison you must go,
  You must go, you must go.
Then off to prison you must go,
  My fair lady.

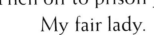

The Grand Old Duke of York

Oh, the grand old Duke of York,
He had ten thousand men.
He marched them up to the top of the hill,
And he marched them down again.
And when they were up, they were up.
And when they were down, they were down,
And when they were only halfway up,
They were neither up nor down!

The Big Ship Sails

The big ship sails on the alley, alley O,
The alley, alley O, the alley, alley O.
The big ship sails on the alley, alley O,
On the last day of September.

The captain said, "It will never, never do,
Never, never do, never, never do."
The captain said, "It will never, never do,"
On the last day of September.

The big ship sank to the bottom of the sea,
The bottom of the sea, the bottom of the sea.
The big ship sank to the bottom of the sea,
On the last day of September.

We all dip our heads in the deep blue sea,
The deep blue sea, the deep blue sea.
We all dip our heads in the deep blue sea,
On the last day of September.

One, Two, Buckle My Shoe

One, two, buckle my shoe,

Three, four, knock at the door.

Five, six, pick up sticks,

Seven, eight, lay them straight.

Nine, ten, a big fat hen,

Eleven, twelve, dig and delve.

Thirteen, fourteen, maids a-courting,

Fifteen, sixteen, maids in the kitchen.

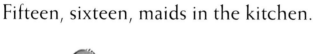

Seventeen, eighteen, maids in waiting,

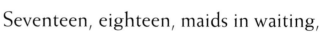

Nineteen, twenty, my plate's empty.

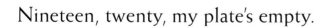

One for the Money

One for the money,
Two for the show,
Three to make ready,
And four to go!

I Love Sixpence

I love sixpence, jolly, jolly sixpence,
    I love sixpence as my life.
I spent a penny of it, I spent a penny of it,
    I took a penny home to my wife.

I love fourpence, jolly, jolly fourpence,
    I love fourpence as my life.
I spent twopence of it, I spent twopence of it,
    I took twopence home to my wife.

I love nothing, jolly, jolly nothing,
    I love nothing as my life.
I spent nothing of it, I spent nothing of it,
    I took nothing home to my wife.

My Father, He Left Me

My father, he left me, just as he was able,
One bowl, one bottle, one table,
Two bowls, two bottles, two tables,
Three bowls, three bottles, three tables,
Four bowls, four bottles, four tables,
Five bowls, five bottles, five tables,
Six bowls, six bottles, six tables.

Hot Cross Buns

Hot cross buns!
Hot cross buns!
One a penny, two a penny,
Hot cross buns!
If your daughters do not like them,
Give them to your sons.
One a penny, two a penny,
Hot cross buns!

Hickety, Pickety

Hickety, pickety, my black hen,
She lays eggs for gentlemen.
Sometimes nine, and sometimes ten,
Hickety, pickety, my black hen.

Chook, Chook, Chook

Chook, chook, chook, chook, chook,
Good morning, Mrs Hen.
How many chickens have you got?
Madam, I've got ten.
Four of them are yellow,
And four of them are brown,
And two of them are speckled red,
The nicest in the town.

Magpies

I saw eight magpies in a tree,
Two for you and six for me.
One for sorrow, two for mirth,
Three for a wedding, four for a birth.
Five for England, six for France,
Seven for a fiddler, eight for a dance.

Jenny Wren

Jenny Wren last week was wed,
And built her nest in Grandpa's shed.
Look in next week and you shall see
Two little eggs, and maybe three.

The Dove Says, Coo, Coo

The dove says, "Coo, coo, what shall I do?
I can scarce maintain two."
"Pooh, pooh," says the wren, "I have got ten,
And keep them all like gentlemen."

Three Blind Mice

Three blind mice,
Three blind mice,
See how they run!
See how they run!
They all ran after the farmer's wife,
Who cut off their tails with a carving knife.
Did you ever see such a sight in your life,
As three blind mice?

White Feet

One white foot, buy him,
Two white feet, try him.
Three white feet, wait and see.
Four white feet, let him be.

Barber, Barber

Barber, barber, shave a pig,
How many hairs to make a wig?
Four and twenty, that's enough.
Give the barber a pinch of snuff.

Gregory Griggs

Gregory Griggs, Gregory Griggs,
Had twenty-seven different wigs.
He wore them up, he wore them down,
To please the people of the town.
He wore them east, he wore them west,
But he never could tell which he loved best.

Three Young Rats

Three young rats with black felt hats,
Three young ducks with new straw flats,
Three young dogs with curling tails,
Three young cats with demi veils,
Went out to walk with two young pigs
In satin vests and sorrel wigs.
But suddenly it chanced to rain,
And so they all went home again.

As I Was Going to St Ives

As I was going to St Ives,
I met a man with seven wives.
Each wife had seven sacks,
Each sack had seven cats,
Each cat had seven kits.
Kits, cats, sacks, wives,
How many were going to St Ives?

(Answer: Only one — "I".)

Five Little Pussy Cats

Five little pussy cats sitting in a row,
Blue ribbons round each neck, fastened in a bow.
Hey, pussies! Ho, pussies! Are your faces clean?
Don't you know you're sitting there so as to be seen?

One, Two, Three, Four, Five

One, two, three, four, five,
Once I caught a fish alive.
Why did you let it go?
Because it bit my finger so.

Six, seven, eight, nine, ten,
Shall we go to fish again?
Not today, some other time,
For I have broke my fishing line.

Three Wise Men

Three wise men of Gotham
Went to sea in a bowl.
If the bowl had been stronger,
My song would be longer!

I Saw Three Ships

I saw three ships come sailing by,
    Come sailing by, come sailing by.
I saw three ships come sailing by,
    On New Year's Day in the morning!

And what do you think was in them then,
    Was in them then, was in them then?
And what do you think was in them then,
    On New Year's Day in the morning?

Three pretty girls were in them then,
    Were in them then, were in them then.
Three pretty girls were in them then,
    On New Year's Day in the morning.

One could whistle and one could sing,
    And one could play the violin.
Such joy there was at my wedding,
    On New Year's Day in the morning!

One Old Oxford Ox

One old Oxford ox opening oysters,

Two toads, totally tired, trying to trot to Tisbury.

Three thick thumping tigers taking toast for tea,

Four finicky fishermen fishing for finny fish.

Five frippery Frenchmen foolishly fishing for frogs,

Six sportsmen shooting snipe.

Seven Severn salmon swallowing shrimps,

Eight eminent Englishmen eagerly examining Europe.

Nine nimble noblemen nibbling nectarines,

Ten tinkering tinkers tinkering ten tin tinderboxes.

Eleven elephants, elegantly equipped,

Twelve typographical topographers typically translating types.

Mary at the Kitchen Door

One, two, three, four,
Mary at the kitchen door.
Five, six, seven, eight,
Eating cherries off a plate.

One's None

One's none,
Two's some,
Three's many,
Four's a penny,
Five's a little hundred.

Three Little Ghostesses

Three little ghostesses,
Sitting on postesses,
Eating buttered toastesses,
Greasing up their fistesses,
Up to their wristesses.
Oh, what beastesses,
To make such feastesses!

One, Two, Three

One, two, three,
I love coffee,
And Billy loves tea.
How good you be,
One, two, three,
I love coffee,
And Billy loves tea.

There Were Three Cooks

There were three cooks of Colebrook,
And they fell out with our cook.
And all was for the pudding he took
From the three cooks of Colebrook.

Four-Leaf Clover

One leaf for fame, one leaf for wealth,
One for a faithful lover,
And one leaf to bring glorious health,
Are all in a four-leaf clover.

One, He Loves

One, he loves; two, he loves;
Three, he loves, they say.
Four, he loves with all his heart;
Five, he casts away.
Six, he loves; seven, she loves;
Eight, they both love.
Nine, he comes; ten, he tarries;
Eleven, he courts; twelve, he marries.

There Were Two Wrens

There were two wrens upon a tree,
Whistle and I'll come to thee.
Another came, and there were three,
Whistle and I'll come to thee.
Another came, and there were four.
You needn't whistle any more,
For, being frightened, off they flew,
And there are none to show to you.

Two Crows

There were two crows sat on a stone,
One flew away and there was one.
The other, seeing his neighbour gone,
He flew away and then there were none.

Two Cats of Kilkenny

There once were two cats of Kilkenny,
Each thought there was one cat too many.
So they fought and they fit,
And they scratched and they bit,
Till, excepting their nails,
And the tips of their tails,
Instead of two cats, there weren't any.

Twelve Huntsmen

Twelve huntsmen with horns and hounds,
Hunting over other men's grounds.

Eleven ships sailing o'er the main,
Some bound for France and some for Spain,
I wish them all safe home again.

Ten comets in the sky,
Some low and some high.

Nine peacocks in the air,
I wonder how they all came there?
I do not know, and I do not care.

Eight joiners in Joiners' Hall,
Working with their tools and all.

Seven lobsters in a dish,
As fresh as any heart could wish.

Six beetles against the wall,
Close by an old woman's apple stall.

Five puppies of our dog Ball,
Who daily for their breakfast call.

Four horses stuck in a bog,
Three monkeys tied to a clog.

Two pudding-ends would choke a dog,

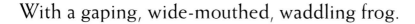

With a gaping, wide-mouthed, waddling frog.

Twinkle, Twinkle

Twinkle, twinkle, little star,
How I wonder what you are!
Up above the world so high,
Like a diamond in the sky.

When the blazing sun is gone,
When he nothing shines upon,
Then you show your little light,
Twinkle, twinkle, all the night.

In the dark blue sky you keep,
And often through my curtains peep,
For you never shut your eye,
Till the sun is in the sky.

Jane Taylor

Star Light

Star light, star bright,
First star I see tonight,
I wish I may, I wish I might,
Have the wish I wish tonight.

I See the Moon

I see the moon,
And the moon sees me.
God bless the moon,
And God bless me.

The Man in the Moon

The Man in the Moon looked out of the moon,
    And this is what he said:
"Now that I'm getting up, 'tis time
    All children went to bed!"

Wee Willie Winkie

Wee Willie Winkie runs through the town,
Upstairs and downstairs in his nightgown,
Rapping at the window, crying through the lock,
"Are the children all in bed, for now it's eight o'clock!"

The Sandman

The Sandman comes,
The Sandman comes.
He has such pretty snow-white sand,
And well he's known throughout the land.
The Sandman comes.

All the Pretty Little Horses

Hush-a-bye, don't you cry,
Go to sleep little baby.
When you wake, you shall have
All the pretty little horses.
Blacks and bays, dapples and greys,
Coach and six little horses.

Bossy-Cow, Bossy-Cow

Bossy-cow, bossy-cow, where do you lie?
In the green meadows, under the sky.

Billy-horse, billy-horse, where do you lie?
Out in the stable, with nobody nigh.

Birdies bright, birdies sweet, where do you lie?
Up in the treetops, ever so high.

Baby dear, baby love, where do you lie?
In my warm cradle, with Mama close by.

Come, Let's to Bed

"Come, let's to bed,"
Says Sleepy-head.
"Tarry awhile," says Slow.
"Put on the pan,"
Says Greedy Nan,
"Let's sup before we go."

A Glass of Milk

A glass of milk and a slice of bread,
And then good night, we must go to bed.

Sippity Sup

Sippity sup, sippity sup,
Bread and milk from a china cup.
Bread and milk from a bright silver spoon,
Made of a piece of the bright silver moon!
Sippity sup, sippity sup,
Sippity, sippity sup!

Go to Bed First

Go to bed first, a golden purse;
Go to bed second, a golden pheasant;
Go to bed third, a golden bird.

Go to Bed Late

Go to bed late,
Stay very small.
Go to bed early,
Grow very tall.

Come to the Window

Come to the window,
My baby, with me,
And look at the stars
That shine on the sea!
There are two little stars
That play at bo-peep
With two little fishes
Far down in the deep,
And two little frogs
Cry, "Neap, neap, neap,
I see a dear baby
That should be asleep!"

Sweet and Low

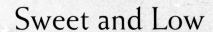

Sweet and low, sweet and low,
    Wind of the western sea.
Low, low, breathe and blow,
    Wind of the western sea!
Over the rolling waters go,
Come from the dying moon, and blow,
    Blow him again to me;
While my little one, while my pretty one, sleeps.

Sleep and rest, sleep and rest,
    Father will come to thee soon;
Rest, rest, on mother's breast,
    Father will come to thee soon.
Father will come to his babe in the nest,
Silver sails all out of the west,
    Under the silver moon;
Sleep, my little one, sleep, my pretty one, sleep.

Alfred, Lord Tennyson

Up the Wooden Hill

Up the wooden hill
    To Bedfordshire,
Down Sheet Lane
    To Blanket Fair.

Diddle, Diddle, Dumpling

Diddle, diddle, dumpling, my son John
Went to bed with his trousers on.
One shoe off, and one shoe on,
Diddle, diddle, dumpling, my son John.

Babyland

How many miles to Babyland?
Anyone can tell.
Up one flight, to your right,
Please to ring the bell.

What do they do in Babyland?
Dream and wake and play,
Laugh and crow, fonder grow,
Jolly times have they.

Rock-a-bye Baby

Rock-a-bye baby, thy cradle is green,
Father's a nobleman, Mother's a queen.
Betty's a lady and wears a gold ring,
And Johnny's a drummer, and drums for the King.

Hush, Little Baby

Hush, little baby, don't say a word,

Papa's going to buy you a mockingbird.

If that mockingbird won't sing,

Papa's going to buy you a diamond ring.

If that diamond ring turns brass,

Papa's going to buy you a looking glass.

If that looking glass gets broke,

Papa's going to buy you a billy goat.

If that billy goat won't pull,

 Papa's going to buy you a cart and bull.

If that cart and bull turn over,

 Papa's going to buy you a dog named Rover.

If that dog named Rover won't bark,

 Papa's going to buy you a horse and cart.

If that horse and cart fall down,

 You'll still be the sweetest little baby in town.

French Cradle Song

If my boy sleep quietly,
He shall see the busy bee,
When it has made its honey fine,
Dancing in the bright sunshine.

If my boy will slumber,
Angels without number
Will draw near, so fair and bright,
For they only come at night.

Sleep, Oh Sleep

Sleep, oh sleep,
While breezes so softly are blowing.
Sleep, oh sleep,
While streamlets so gently are flowing.
Sleep, oh sleep!

Sleep, oh sleep,
While birds in the forest are singing.
Sleep, oh sleep,
While echoes with music are ringing.
Sleep, oh sleep!

Sleep, oh sleep,
While angels are watching beside thee.
Sleep, oh sleep,
May blessings for ever betide thee.
Sleep, oh sleep.

Hush-a-bye, Baby

Hush-a-bye, baby, lie still in the cradle,
Mother has gone to buy a soup ladle.
When she comes back, she'll bring us some meat,
And Father and baby shall have some to eat.

Dear Baby, Lie Still

Hush-a-bye, baby, lie still with thy daddy,
Thy mammy has gone to the mill,
To get some meal, to make a cake,
So pray, my dear baby, lie still.

Rock-a-bye, Baby, Rock

Rock-a-bye, baby, rock, rock, rock,
Baby shall have a new pink frock!
A new pink frock and a ribbon to tie,
If baby is good and does not cry.

Rock-a-bye, baby, rock, rock, rock,
Listen, who comes with a knock, knock, knock?
Oh, it is pussy! Come in, come in!
Mother and baby are always at home.

Raisins and Almonds

To my baby's cradle in the night
Comes a little goat all snowy-white.
The goat will trot to the market,
While Mother her watch does keep,
Bringing back raisins and almonds.
Sleep, my little one, sleep.

Hush-a-bye, Baby, on the Treetop

Hush-a-bye, baby, on the treetop,
When the wind blows, the cradle will rock.
When the bough breaks, the cradle will fall,
And down will come baby, cradle and all.

Sleep, Baby, Sleep

Sleep, baby, sleep,
Thy father guards the sheep,
Thy mother shakes the dreamland tree,
And from it fall sweet dreams for thee.
Sleep, baby, sleep.

Sleep, baby, sleep,
Our cottage vale is deep.
The little lamb is on the green,
With woolly fleece so soft and clean.
Sleep, baby, sleep.

Sleep, baby, sleep,
Down where the woodbines creep.
Be always like the lamb so mild,
A kind and sweet and gentle child.
Sleep, baby, sleep.

Cradle Song

Lullaby and good night, with roses bedight,
With lilies bedecked is baby's wee bed.
Lay thee down now and rest,
May thy slumber be blessed.
Lay thee down now and rest,
May thy slumber be blessed.

Lullaby and good night, thy mother's delight,
Bright angels around my darling shall stand.
They will guard thee from harms,
Thou shalt wake in my arms.
They will guard thee from harms,
Thou shalt wake in my arms.

Johannes Brahms

The Evening Is Coming

The evening is coming, the sun sinks to rest,
The birds are all flying straight home to the nest.
"Caw," says the crow as he flies overhead,
"It's time little children were going to bed!"

The butterfly, drowsy, has folded its wing.
The bees are returning, no more the birds sing.
Their labour is over, their nestlings are fed.
It's time little children were going to bed.

Here comes the pony, his work is all done,
Down through the meadow he takes a good run.
Up go his heels and down goes his head.
It's time little children were going to bed.

Now the Day Is Over

Now the day is over,
Night is drawing nigh.
Shadows of the evening
Steal across the sky.

Down with the Lambs

Down with the lambs,
      Up with the lark,
Run to bed, children,
      Before it gets dark.

Quiet the Night

Quiet the night,
Soft is the breeze.
Dim is the light
Of the faraway moon.

Sleep, children, sleep,
Be not alarmed,
Angels on guard
Will keep you unharmed.

Golden Slumbers

Golden slumbers kiss your eyes,
Smiles awake you when you rise.
Sleep, pretty baby, do not cry,
And I will sing you a lullaby.
Rock them, rock them, lullaby.

Good Night

Good night,
Sleep tight,
Wake up bright
In the morning light
To do what's right
With all your might.